Floyd B. Johnson is an educator, politician, committed father, and a respected leader in Dayton, Ohio. Special thanks for him allowing me to share our family experiences, which he created.

Many thanks to Nancy Mayes, Alfred Johnson, Gloria White, and Earnestine Smith for their encouragement. My children, Cicely, Garren, and my granddaughter, Aaliyah, thanks for the memories.

Special thanks to my sister, Jewel Jones, and my friend, Marcia Norton, for editing and inspiring me to continue using my gift of storytelling.

www.mascotbooks.com

Floyd B's Pond

For more information, please contact:
Mascot Books
560 Herndon Parkway #120
Herndon, VA 20170
info@mascotbooks.com

CPSIA Code: PRT0714A
ISBN-13: 9781620866993

Printed in the United States

Floyd B's
Pond

Mary J. Grant

illustrated by **James Balkovek**

Squeak, squeak went the bright red wagon that was full of rocks and sticks. As soon as the children in the neighborhood heard the *squeak, squeak*, they knew it was Floyd B. His name was Floyd Benny, but everyone called him Floyd B. He was a tall, thin, shorthaired, twelve-year-old boy who was very curious. He enjoyed playing with his pet rabbit, turtle, and all kinds of games. But most of all, he liked being creative. Science was very exciting to him. He could not wait for school to start so that he could do his seventh grade science fair project.

Floyd B had a younger sister named Maymay. Her real name was Mary, but everyone in the neighborhood called her Maymay. She was very shy, but she loved to talk about her big brother. She felt special having a big brother.

Regina was their five-year-old cousin who lived in the upstairs, two-bedroom flat. Maymay and Regina were both in the first grade and they played together every day.

When school started, Floyd B's science teacher, Mr. Curtis, said what Floyd B waited all summer to hear. It was time for the students to begin their science fair projects. Floyd B decided to make a fish pond in his backyard for his project. He wanted this project to be very special.

Mr. Curtis wanted to see the science fair project outlines in October. When Mr. Curtis announced that the first-place winner would receive a trophy, Floyd B was so excited, he felt as though he couldn't breathe fast enough. He barely heard him say special awards would be given for second and third places or that everyone would receive a certificate of participation.

When Floyd B turned in his science fair project outline to Mr. Curtis, he said, "Mr. Curtis, I want to win the first place trophy."

Mr. Curtis smiled and said, "Anything worth doing is worth doing well. That means work hard and it will pay off."

Floyd B had the biggest smile a boy could have when Mr. Curtis said those magical words. He always made Floyd B feel special. Floyd B felt like Mr. Curtis had just given him the secret to winning the first place trophy. He always worked hard to do well in his science class; but now, he would work even harder after hearing Mr. Curtis' advice.

When Floyd B got home after school, he got a shovel and started to dig a hole in his backyard. He dug until he had a hole as big and wide as he was tall.

Maymay asked, "Can we help?"

"No," Floyd B said.

Floyd B had a book that gave him directions on how to build the fish pond. The book had easy steps to follow with pictures of all kinds of species of fish, beautiful lily pads, and flowers.

Floyd B said, "I am going to the lake at Lakeside Park to get some goldfish." Lakeside Park was a man-made lake on Germantown Hill, not far from where they lived.

Jumping up and down, Maymay and Regina asked, "Can we go too? Can we go, please?"

Floyd B said, "No, I will let you see my goldfish tomorrow!"

Floyd B walked away with his red wagon, *squeak*, *squeak*, as he went up the hill and met his friend. Maymay and Regina watched until they could not see him anymore. They played with their toys and went inside to eat.

Mother said, "Where is Floyd B? I sent him to the store, but he hasn't come back yet."

Maymay said, "Floyd B went to Lakeside Park with his friend to get some goldfish."

Regina said, "Ohhhh, you should not have told on him."

Mother said, "Oh, just wait until he comes back!"

Maymay and Regina looked at Mother and they knew by the look on her face that Floyd B was in BIG trouble.

They waited for Floyd B to come home. At last, just before dark, Floyd B came home with two goldfish that he had gotten from the lake. He was in r-e-a-l-l-y BIG trouble.

Maymay said, "I told you to let us go with you. I'm sorry you are in trouble." She walked away with a sad look on her face. She thought it was her fault that her brother was in trouble.

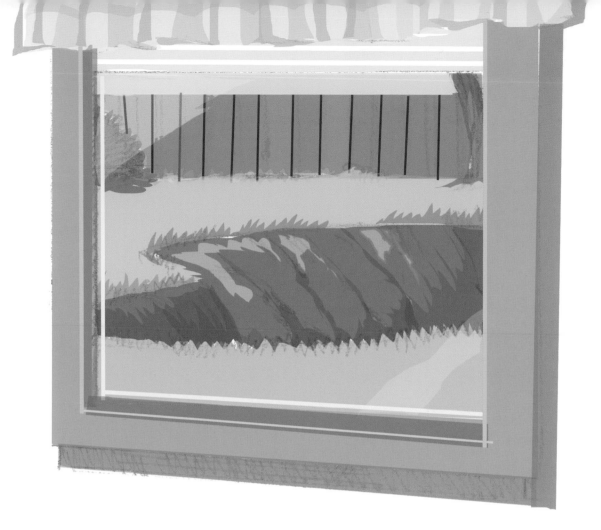

The next day, Floyd B could not go outside. He sat looking out the back window at the big hole he had dug. He had a lot of time to plan his goldfish pond. He drew a picture of what the pond would look like when finished. The picture showed a waterfall with many colorful rocks arranged around the edge of the pond. The picture had wire around the edge with small holes for flowers growing from lily pads.

When their daddy came home, Maymay said, "Daddy! Daddy! Floyd B dug a hole in the backyard!"

Daddy asked, "Where is Floyd B?"

Floyd B's daddy was very upset about the big hole in the backyard. He had no idea what Floyd B was going to do in the backyard.

Daddy said, "Floyd B, you should never dig holes in the ground without permission."

"Okay, Daddy," Floyd B said in a sad voice. "May I please build a fish pond for my science fair project?" he asked.

"Yes, but let this be a lesson for you, son," Daddy said in his deep voice.

Floyd B worked hard, just like Mr. Curtis told him, trying to make the pond look like the picture. He mixed some of his daddy's cement and poured it on the bottom. Sticks and rocks of all sizes were placed very carefully in the cement.

After two days, the cement in the goldfish pond was dry. Floyd B went to the faucet on the side of the house and connected the water hose. He carefully filled the pond with water and placed the two goldfish into it. The fish swam back and forth. *Splash, splash, trickle, ripple, gurgle, swish* went the water as the fish swam around and around. Floyd B placed the metal wire around the edge of the pond. He fastened the edges of the wire in a circle to make sure small animals would not eat the fish.

The next day, Maymay called, "Regina, come downstairs!"

She came running down the stairs. "Wha-a-a-t!" she asked in a loud, excited voice.

"Look what Floyd B has done!" Maymay said.

Maymay and Regina enjoyed looking at the fish every day. Maymay said, "Let's name one goldfish Goldy because it is gold and shiny."

Regina said, "Let's name the other fish Flakey because the fins look like cornflakes."

Floyd B agreed that these were good names. He said, "I am going back to Lakeside to get some lily pads." He went into the house and asked his mother if he could go.

Jumping up and down, Maymay and Regina asked, "Can we go, please?"

Floyd B said, "No, I will show you tomorrow!" Floyd B walked away with his red wagon going *squeak, squeak,* as he went up the hill and met his friend, James.

The next day Maymay went to the goldfish pond. Floyd B was sitting on some big rocks, looking at the lily pads.

Maymay called, "Regina! Come and see the goldfish pond!"

Floyd B said, "These are called lily pads, and they grow flowers." The lily pads had small flowers and made the pond look very pretty. It was a beautiful home for Goldy and Flakey. "Sometimes, the fish use lily pads for food."

As they sat watching Goldy and Flakey, Maymay said, "Look! There is a tail coming out of the dirt. Is that another fish?"

Floyd B said, "That is not a fish, it is a tadpole."

Regina said, "Wow, this is a great pond. Floyd B, why don't you shape the big rocks into chairs?"

"Okay," he said. Floyd B and James pushed the big rocks into shapes. Floyd B took pictures of the pond for his project and put it in his journal.

Soon, the days were getting colder because winter was coming. Maymay and Regina wondered what was going to happen to Goldy and Flakey in the cold weather.

After school Maymay said, "Look! The tadpole looks different."

Floyd B said, "It is not a tadpole anymore. Now, it is a frog."

They watched as the frog jumped from one lily pad to another. Each day, the lily pads opened in the morning and closed at nighttime.

"Come, Goldy and Flakey!" said Maymay and Regina as they held their hands out with the fish food. The fish came very quickly.

As the days began to shorten, snow covered the pond. "What will Goldy and Flakey do?" Maymay asked Regina in a sad, sad voice.

Ice covered the pond during the winter. Maymay and Regina went outside with their hats and winter coats on, trying to look into the fish pond, but they could not see anything. "What are Goldy and Flakey doing?" asked Regina.

They visited the pond every day after school all winter long.

Floyd B took pictures and wrote in his fish pond journal every week. On the front of his journal, he wrote his hypothesis: <u>Goldfish Can Survive in a Pond in the Cold Climate During the Winter</u>. He shared his project with the girls.

Maymay asked, "What is a hypothesis?"

Floyd B said, "A hypothesis is a statement that you have to prove."

Spring came and the goldfish pond started to melt. Floyd B took pictures of the melting ice and the goldfish. He put the pictures and his journal information on a board and took it to school.

A week later after school, Floyd B came running into the house shouting, "I won! I won!"

Mother asked, "What is all that noise?"

"See my trophy and first place ribbon!" he shouted in an excited voice.

When Maymay came home from school, she yelled, "Regina, come and see this!"

Regina came running down the stairs with her books in hand. She dropped the books and said, "Wha-a-at!"

Maymay said, "Look what Floyd B won!"

"Wow! Look at that big trophy," Regina screamed.

Maymay and Regina settled down on the big rock, watching the fish. They were bigger this year. Floyd B had prepared a really nice board with all of the pictures, information about the goldfish, and how they had survived over the winter.

Floyd B said, "The fish hibernated."

Maymay and Regina said, "Hibernate together!"

During the winter, the goldfish did not swim. They burrowed deep in the bottom of the pond. There they lay close to the rocks and mud. The rocks and the mud covered them and helped the fish stay alive. Nature took care of them while they slept during the winter.

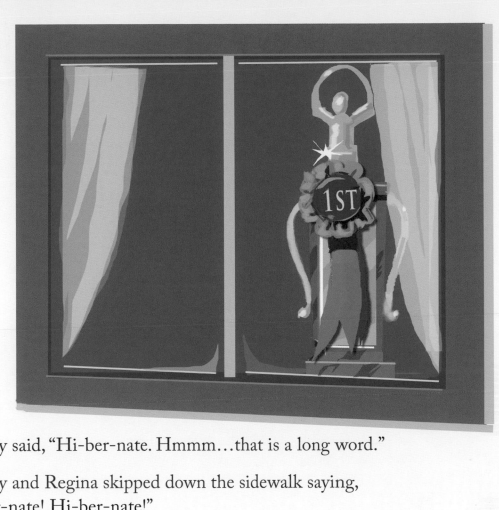

Maymay said, "Hi-ber-nate. Hmmm…that is a long word."

Maymay and Regina skipped down the sidewalk saying,
"Hi-ber-nate! Hi-ber-nate!"

They took the jump rope, made up a song, and began to jump.

> *Hibernate, hibernate,*
> *Winter comes,*
> *Time to sleep,*
> *Hibernate, hibernate,*
> *And wait for spring.*

Each year, the fish grew bigger. The lily pads were prettier as the green algae grew. The fish pond became a meeting place for all the children in the neighborhood.

Regina and Maymay enjoyed sitting at their favorite place: Floyd B's fish pond.

Many families like the Johnsons, Nelsons, Rosses, Browns, Hendersons, Bennetts, and a host of other neighbors all remembered the fun they had at Floyd B's fish pond.

About the Author

Mary Johnson Grant is an educator and storyteller who enjoys sharing her childhood experiences. She is the author of the children's book *My Daddy Taught Me To Read*, a true story of her growing up in Dayton, Ohio.

www.storiesbymary.com

marygrant@gmail.com

Hibernate
A Jump Rope Rhyme

Hibernate, hibernate,
Winter comes,
Time to sleep,
Hibernate, hibernate,
And wait for spring.

Have a book idea?

Contact us at:

Mascot Books

560 Herndon Parkway

Suite 120

Herndon, VA

info@mascotbooks.com | www.mascotbooks.com